Reflections of Me

Chelley

Prologue

Tyree

"What you doing on my corner, lil man?" I rolled the back window down and asked the kid who was standing on one of my appointed blocks. He looked to be about fourteen-years-old, and that was fucking with my head. I had a lot of young niggas working for me, but they were all over eighteen-years-old. They were all grown and could make their own decisions. This kid had to be desperate for something.

"What? You dumb or something? You can't be blind, you looking dead at me. I'm working."

He couldn't have known who I was if he was talking to me like that, so I let it slide with a chuckle.

"Get in the car, lil man." My driver unlocked the doors to grant him access inside. The kid remained where he stood. He looked away from the Escalade and didn't budge. "I'm Ty," I informed him. "You work for me," I added with an aggressive pat to my chest.

I finally caught his attention with that one. Leaving the block, he rounded the truck and got in on the left side. His clothes were baggy, swallowing him whole. He was working for a purpose. It was evident that he was working on the block to eat.

"Circle the block a few times, E," I told my driver. I needed time to figure him out. "Drive slow."

"My bad, man. I didn't know…"

"I didn't expect you to. I usually associate by name. Not many know my face. I run shit behind the scenes."

"I… I didn't mean to disrespect you," he said.

"How old are you, young?"

"Fourteen," he answered quickly. Just like I thought. He was too young to be hustling. I wanted to ask who recruited him, but I could figure that out on my own.

"How much do you need to keep you off the block?" I pulled a wad of cash from my pocket and started counting out the bills. I'd been where he was. I would never forget being the hungry kid who just wanted to help my mom make ends meet.

"I don't want your money." He scoffed. "I rather work for mine." He wiped beads of sweat from his forehead. Georgia's heat in the summer wasn't a game. His dark brown skin was melting, making me wonder how long he'd been out there today.

"Yo. Turn the air up, E." E looked at me through the rear-view mirror and nodded. Cold air blasted in the backseat, cooling the young kid down. "What's your name?"

"Josh," he admitted after long moments of silence. "Joshua Stevens."

"Where you live, Josh?"

"Look, man. Just let me out and I'll walk home from here. I don't want my sister to know about this. I'm just trying to help her out. She's been taking care of me and my little brothers since our parents were hit in a drive by shooting."

"Don't make me ask you again, young."

"I live on Golden Rod. It's eight blocks from here."

"You heard the man, E."

E sped up to head in the direction of his crib. I slouched in my seat and brushed my hand over my face. Situations like this fucked me up.

I'd been in his shoes. My parents had been

locked up all my life. They would be locked up until God took them home. I had to fend for myself and my little sister. There were no lengths I wouldn't go to take care of her.

Josh threw his head against the headrest and huffed. "My sister is going to kill me," he mumbled.

"No, she won't." I chuckled. "I got your back."

I didn't know what the fuck I was doing. I usually minded my business and kept it pushing. Today I felt inclined to help the kid. I saw myself inside of him.

He was quiet during the ride to his house. He pulled his phone from his pocket a few times, and then stashed it back in there like there was no use for it.

Josh coughed to muffle the sound of his growling stomach, but it was too late, I'd heard it.

I never felt sorry for hungry men who could get off their ass and hustle, but Josh was only a kid. The circumstances against him weren't fair.

"I think I heard about your parents. This happened last year?" I asked. Albany was a small city in Georgia. Almost everyone knew of everyone, and news traveled fast. Especially tragic news. We didn't need news channels to spread the word; the people of the town did a better job at telling it all.

Josh responded to my question by nodding. Tears formed in his eyes, but he wiped them away quick and put his poker face back on.

"A year and five days," he clarified. "Shit still isn't easy to deal with."

"I can only imagine." I glanced out the window and sighed. I barely knew him. That didn't stop me from feeling for him. "Who put you on?" It was a long shot to ask him. If he was the type of kid I thought he was, he wouldn't release any information to me. It was street code. Him being in trouble didn't matter. If it was instilled in him not to run his mouth, he wouldn't, no matter who I was. Whether it was life or death, he wouldn't utter a word about who put him on.

"I'm out here on my own," he said. It was a convincing lie that made me chuckle.

"Yeah, aight," I returned and left it alone. He knew my name and who he worked for but tried to convince me he was out there on his own. I respected his pride to take on the punishment on his own.

"That's my house right there." He pointed to the brightest house on the street.

My driver pulled alongside the curb in front of it and parked. Josh pleaded for me not to get out when I reached for the door handle.

"C'mon, man. I won't go back out there.

Just don't tell my sister."

I looked in his eyes and felt sorry for him. Josh went in his pocket to hand me the wad of cash he'd made today, and I denied it.

"I don't want your money, young. You made that on your own, remember?" He nodded slowly and dropped his head. "Keep your head up at all times."

He followed suit when I got out the car. I assumed his sister was home because a Honda Civic was parked in the driveway.

"I got you, aight? Don't trip." I patted his chest when he caught up to me. I was six-five in height and he was almost there. By the time he'd reached his prime, he would be taller than me.

I looked up when he cleared his throat. His sister had opened the door and stood in front of it with a frown on her face. She looked to be a mixture of angry and relieved to see him.

"You better have a good got damn reason on why I pay over eighty dollars a month for that iPhone when you don't know how to answer it," she said. We hadn't gotten the chance to walk up the steps to the porch before she started. "I've been calling you all fucking day, Josh. You know you have chores on Saturdays. Where the hell have you been?"

"Aella... I..." Josh stuttered to explain.

"You better not lie to me either! And who the fuck is this?" She folded her arms and rolled her eyes at me.

I chuckled and bit my tongue. I understood her anger, so I let her get it out. Besides that, she was beautiful as fuck. How good she looked caught me off guard. Aella stood by the front door in dark denim shorts and a white crop-top. Her thighs were the thickest thing on her. Her waist was tight. She had a real coke bottle shape that impressed me and my dick. My dick jumped at the sight of her. I couldn't have helped that shit if I tried.

"How you doing, Aella? I'm Ty."

"Yeah." She rolled her eyes. "I thought you looked familiar."

I didn't know her and she damn sure didn't know me. The look on my face told her I was confused.

"Get in the house, Josh." She motioned him inside and closed him in there after he entered. I approached the porch slowly and ascended the stairs to properly greet her. I held my hand out for hers, but to no avail, because Aella wasn't budging. Neither was the frown on her beautiful face.

"You think you know me?" I slanted my eyes at her while wondering if she really did.

"I know of you. I've seen a rare picture of the infamous face you rarely show around you. I know you run the streets that I don't need my little brother on."

"Aye, it's not like that. I was bringing him home to get him off my streets." I couldn't deny anything else she'd said. She was right when she said she knew of me. She seemed to have her facts down packed thus far.

"I'm supposed to trust that?"

"It's up to you." I shrugged.

Aella rolled her hazel eyes at me and waved me off.

"I need you to stay off my streets too," I added.

It all began to come together for her as she stared at me on edge. Finding Josh on my streets was a shock. I didn't believe in recruiting kids.

Aella on the other hand, had been on my radar for a minute. She'd caught my eye one night at a block party some months back. I never thought I would see her again until E was driving me around my blocks and I spotted her. I'd had plans to confront her about it for two weeks now. After finding Josh, I realized they were trying to survive. For reasons unknown outside of needing a meal, they were out on the block without each other's knowledge, doing whatever they could to fend for their family.

"Excuse me?" She put her hand on her hip and looked me upside my head.

"You heard me, Aella."

There was nothing more I needed to say than that. I turned around and headed back to the truck. Aella eyes were still trained on me. I felt them burning a hole in my back. I felt them until I got in the back of the escalade and she couldn't see me behind the tints anymore.

"That's her?" E looked at me through the rear-view mirror and asked. He wasn't only my driver, he was my partner. My best friend.

"Yeah." I chuckled. "That's her pretty ass. She has a mouth on her too. I knew she would."

"You get her number?"

"Nah. She was talking too much shit for me today. I'll see her again," I said. I was certain I would see her again. A woman like that didn't take orders from anyone, not even the nigga who ran the streets she'd been serving on. I understood she had a family to feed, but she didn't need to be out there like that. I was going to find out who put her and her little brother on. And when I saw her again, I was going to make her mine and take care of her.

"All this time you've had your eye on her, and you ain't got her number?" E shook his head and pulled off. He sped down the road scoffing at me.

"Man chill out. I'll get it. Timing is important."

E let it go and focused on the road ahead of him. I was grateful for the silence to think about what had just happened. I'd been scoping her beautiful ass out for a while. That was the closest I'd come to her and I was raving over that shit. Aella was a stunning woman. After one look at her, I could tell she was the type of woman I needed in my life. Men respected her when they saw her out. They knew she could hold her own. That was only one of the many reasons I wanted her on my arm.

"I'm going to get her, E. Trust me." I sighed. Seeing her humbled me every time. I was a hard-headed ass nigga until I saw her. She had the ability to soften me, and she didn't even know it. I didn't mean shit to her yet, and already, she meant everything to me.

"I gotta get her," I mumbled to myself.

Chapter One

Aella

"Are you fucking kidding me, Josh!?" I slammed the front door of our house and stomped upstairs to his room. "Stay down here boys," I told my younger, twin brothers, Chase and Chaz. I'd never let them see me upset before. After our parents were killed in a drive-by shooting with bullets that didn't belong to them, I put my best face forward for my brothers. Especially the six-year old's. I tried to always have them see me with a smile on my face. I adored all three of my younger brothers. Unfortunately, the fourteen-year-old menace thought he was grown. My parents were probably rolling over in their grave right now over his actions!

Our parents' bedroom door was wide open. Josh went in there every day to get a feel for them, and I hadn't been in there since they were alive last year. I moved back into my childhood home to take care of them in a home we were all used to, but I had to admit, it was hard being here without our parents. Hard living without our parents, in general.

"You need to stop all that cursing, Aella," Josh said. The nerve of him. His bushy eyebrow having tail had a slick mouth and I couldn't deny he'd gotten it from me. "Mom and dad wouldn't like that."

"Mom and dad wouldn't like you being out there selling drugs either. Now would they? What do you think you are doing, Josh?"

"I'm helping you! You can't take care of all of us with no help! I know you're doing the best you can. You work them fast food jobs you hate because you had to drop out of nursing school and come back to Georgia to take care of us."

"Josh, things will get better for us. You have

to believe that. And you have to focus on school and stay out of trouble."

He felt bad for me. I knew he hated that I dropped out of college to come back home. Josh was very intelligent for his age. He knew very well how much school meant to me. Since a little girl, I'd wanted to be a nurse. He felt guilty that I had to put a stop to my dream to come home. I despised that logic.

"Why is school important? School doesn't help you pay the bills." He pulled a wad of money from his pocket and tossed it in my folded arms. Without counting it, I assumed it was a good five thousand dollars or more. I wondered how long he'd been saving it. Just how long had he been in the streets!

"Josh." I rolled the money between my palm and fingers and sighed. "This is dirty money. Yeah, it's good for a little while. And yes, it will help pay the bills, but your freedom isn't worth this. It would break my heart if you got caught up and went to jail… or worse."

"Juvie ain't nothing." He shrugged. "I can handle that."

"Can you please listen to me, J." I was trying to maintain my patience with him, but he was running me thin. "I wouldn't be able to handle. We need you here. I need your help with your brothers so please just... listen to me."

"Alright," he mumbled and huffed. "I'll leave it alone."

"You promise you'll stay out of trouble?"

"Yes. I promise."

"Good." I approached him for a hug. After squeezing him in my arms tightly, I stepped back and glared at him. "Because if you ever try that shit again, I'll beat your ass myself. The way mom and dad should've beaten your bad ass a long time ago."

I exited his room and rushed downstairs to check on the twins. They were exactly where I'd left them, playing with their Legos.

"Dinner will be ready soon!" I shouted to everyone as I made my way into the kitchen. I stashed the wad of money Josh tossed at me in the pocket of my jean shorts and shook my head.

Life was kicking my ass in every way. Hard punches to my gut were coming in at all angles. A year had passed since my parents' demise and it felt like the first day every morning I woke up. One day I would wake up and it would hurt less, but right now, it hurt more and more every day.

"How does pizza sound?" I shouted again. I wasn't in the mood to cook anything.

"Yes!" The twins cheered.

"Wings too," Josh shouted from upstairs.

I loved my brothers with everything inside of me. Protecting them at all cost was my main priority. If I ever lost them, I wouldn't know how to be strong anymore.

"Pizza and wings it is," I said.

As I scrolled through my phone to find my favorite delivery app, Tyree Lawson's threat lingered in my head. He was gentle with me, and his eyes scanned my body like he wanted me. Still, I took his mini threat serious. Everyone knew about him. His name rang bells around the city. When he advised you to do something or to stop doing something, taking heed to his request was the right thing to do. Tyree wasn't to be toyed with.

He didn't scare me at all. If anything, he intrigued me. Tyree was a mystery I wanted to learn more about. I wanted to turn him into an open book at my will.

Shaking my thoughts of him away, I focused on ordering pizza and wings, then cleaned the dining area to prepare to eat with my brothers. I was sure I would see him again, but for now, my brothers needed my love and support after the day we'd all had.

***

At only twenty-five years old, my life was in shambles. My parents had left me with the most important job there was. I was the legal guardian of my brothers and that title was driving me crazy.

"I suck at this," I vented to my best friend, Danielle while sitting in my car. It was going on two in the morning and I didn't want to wake my brothers up. Josh was a light sleeper who always caught me crying. Crying in my car was the only safe place to get it out.

"No, you don't," Danielle almost shouted at

me. "You're doing the best you can. Shit. The best you know how to do. You hardly have family that isn't self-absorbed or in jail, and you're doing all of this on your own. Give yourself more credit."

"Josh got caught selling drugs today. He got caught doing that shit on Tyree's turf. I yelled at him for it, but it didn't feel right. I'm a hypocrite. And Tyree made sure to tell us he doesn't want either of us on his blocks."

"He said that?" Danielle gasped.

"In so many words, yes."

"Damn, girl." Danielle sighed. "You know I will help you with whatever..."

"Yes, I know, but I don't want your help. You have your own problems."

"Don't we all!" Danielle shouted. "That doesn't matter to me. What matters to me is that you and your brothers are safe and have all you need. When you fall short, I can help you. You're my best friend and you would do the same for me. Wouldn't you?"

"Yes." I nodded like she could see me. Danielle and I had been close friends since high school. There wasn't anything we wouldn't do for each other, so I couldn't argue with her.

"Okay then. What do you need?"

"We'll be fine for a while, Dani. Thank you."

"You don't have to thank me. I'm here for you. Always. I love you."

"I love you too." I smiled and wiped tears from my eyes. Danielle was a gem during a time like this. She'd been there for me every step of the way.

"What else did Tyree say?" She randomly asked.

"It's less about what he said and how he looked at me, trust me." She probably had no idea what I meant, but I knew very well. There was more he wanted to say to me. His eyes exposed him, and something told me that wasn't the last I would see of him.

"He could look at me however he wants," Danielle joked. "That's one fine man."

"He's okay." I giggled.

Truthfully, he was a beautiful man. Tyree was tall, undeniably handsome and charming. His teeth were pearly white, and his smile looked like a model's smile straight out of a magazine. If you'd ever seen a man who looked too fine to be touched, he could definitely relate to Tyree Lawson. His beard was thick and inviting. Talk about a damn distraction. I had to focus on the real problem at hand to be strong around Tyree. That's how fine he was.

"Whatever, girl. You can sleep on him all you want, but we both know the truth," Danielle said. She was right, and I couldn't go against the truth.

"How are you and Desmond doing?" I asked. Desmond was her long-time boyfriend. Three years to be exact. I was sure he wouldn't be keen on her lusting over other men.

"We're doing." She scoffed. "He's always working and I'm always home alone. The usual."

"Aww, Dani. I'm sorry to hear that. Have you talked to him about it yet?"

"No use. His career is important to him. More important to him than I am."

"You don't know that."

"It's what he's shown me, Aella. I can only go by his actions. Fuck everything else. He can't keep trying to please me with sweet nothings," she said. "And don't be sorry. Men can only do to us what we accept from them. I've let him put his career before me for far too long."

I sat in my car with the doors locked and listened to Danielle vent. I didn't mind being there for her, for once. It was a nice change and diversion from my own problems that I couldn't seem to escape.

While I tried to listen with undivided attention, it was hard. My introduction to Tyree was taking over my mind. Who did he think he was? I knew he possessed a lot of power but if he thought he could show up and call the shots, he was wrong. Nevertheless, I was grateful for him and owed him a thousand 'thank you's'. He'd brought my brother to me and took him off the streets. He'd proven I needed to pay more attention to Josh and the things he was doing. For that, I was grateful. I'd feared something was wrong with him when a black Escalade pulled in front of our house.

I feared a knock on the door with bad news. Imagine my surprise seeing the infamous Tyree with my brother. I would have to remember to thank him when I saw him again. And I knew I would. I would see him again. Someway. Somehow.

Chapter Two

Tyree

The next day, E drove me around my blocks while I was in deep thought. Shaking Aella was impossible. She was heavy on my mind because I wanted to help her. Even Josh was popping up in my head nonstop.

I wasn't in the business of saving people. I worked hard for everything I had, making sure not to accept any handouts and to take care of my own. I got my little sister out the hood by paying her way through college right after she graduated. I wasn't going to risk letting her jump head first into any type of street shit.

"Aye, that's her coming out of Gina's?" E pointed Aella out. She was coming out of a popular food joint with a bag in her hand. Her hair was in a bun on top of her head and a beautiful smile was plastered on her face. I knew I would peep her again.

"Stop in front of the restaurant," I instructed him. Once he did as I said, I opened the backdoor and stepped out. Her hazel eyes landed on me immediately. Aella looked ahead at me impressed and shocked altogether.

"What? Are you stalking me now?" She rolled her neck and her eyes.

"Not yet." I shrugged. "You the only one who can get something to eat around here? I like Gina's too."

"Boy you know damn well you weren't worried about Gina's. Besides, I eat her every other day and I never see you here." Aella started for her car, and I followed closely behind. She had my attention now, and I needed her to know that.

"Aella," I called out to her. She stopped in front of her car and leaned on it.

"Can I help you with something?" She sassed.

"You always this mean?"

"No. I'm usually nice. But when men show up at my doorstep with bad news and threats, I change faces."

"I helped your brother. I brought him home to you."

"I appreciate that part of it," she said. I stopped her before she could pull on the door handle of her car.

"Can I talk to you?"

"You're talking right now," she returned with an attitude. "And you aren't saying much."

"When can I take you out?" I asked, coming right out with it. There was a better way I could've asked her, but her mean ass wasn't giving me time to get it out.

Aella scoffed and shook her head. "You want to take me out? Me?"

"Why is that so hard to believe?" I wondered aloud. Maybe she didn't see what I saw in her. I didn't know what her question really meant. All I knew was, I wanted to take her out. I wanted to know all there was to know about her.

"I don't know. I just wasn't expecting that."

"So, what do you say?" I shrugged and focused on her face. It softened by the minute. After stashing her food on the backseat of her car, she closed the door and turned back around to face me.

"I hardly have time to go on a date," she said. "I take care of my brothers. There's three of them."

"I know how many brothers you have, Aella. I've done my research on you."

"You don't think that's insane?" She side-eyed me and laughed.

"Not really. When I'm interested in a woman, I do what I have to do to get to know them."

Aella looked me up and down and held back from blushing. Her brown cheeks lifted without her permission. I hated it whenever she looked away from me. I loved looking into her hazel eyes in hopes of figuring her out.

"Tyree…" She paused when she noticed me smiling like a fool. 'What?"

"Nothing. Say what you have to say. I just like how you say my name n'shit."

"Boy. If you don't…"

I approached her before she could finish. Towering over her with a smirk. I summoned her eyes by lifting her chin with my index finger.

"I'm a grown ass man. Trust me," I assured. "So, what do you say?"

She took a while to answer, but eventually, she gave in to what I wanted.

"Okay," she whispered.

Digging in my pocket for my phone, I pulled it out and handed it to her. I needed access to her in more ways than one. Driving around my blocks hoping I saw her again wasn't enough.

Aella stored her number and handed it back to me with a faint smile. She batted her lashes and circled her car to get behind the wheel.

"Hopefully I'll see you later," her sweet voice said before she pulled off.

"You will," I said, following her car with my eyes. I hoped she read my lips, because she would definitely see me later.

***

"Clean this shit up!" I walked in one of my trap houses and started kicking shit over. The niggas that worked for me were disgusting and messy as fuck. Some of them were nineteen years old, fresh out of school and confused as ever. They didn't know what to do with themselves, they only knew they needed money to survive. Just like I'd directed Josh the other way, I should've denied putting them on. It was a different ballgame when they were grown, though. The decision was up to them.

"How many times I have to tell you muthafuckers that cleanness is the closest thing to Godliness?" I shouted.

"Here he go," one of them mumbled from the back of the room.

Without having to ask who was brave enough to say that shit to me, everyone in the room faced Trent and made it easier for me.

"I should've known," I hissed. I saw myself pulling out my gun and slapping his overgrown ass in the face with it. His lip would've busted and stopped him from talking so much shit and his nose would've broken and humbled him.

Seeing Aella had me on a calm tip, so I let it slide this once. I dismissed everyone from the trap house with a demand to hustle and report back to me later on.

"Except you." I stopped Trent from leaving by pushing him back and patting his chest. He pierced his eyes at me, then stepped back when he feared I would hit him. "Stay back and clean this place up."

"Me?"

"Ain't nobody else in the room, my nigga. Yes, you! Is there a problem?"

"Naw," he mumbled again.

"What's up?" I questioned, wanting him to speak up.

"There's no problem," he said, this time loud enough for me to hear him clearly.

"Sounds about right." I threw my hand up and left out the trap without another word.

E was in the Escalade waiting on me to hop back in. All I could think about when I got inside was where I was taking her. I had no plan in mind other than simply being around her again.

"Where to, Boss?" E questioned before he pulled off.

"Home," I said. "I got a date tonight, E." I rubbed my hands together and licked my lips. "I think I'm going to get behind the wheel of one of my cars tonight for this one."

"I don't blame you, man. She seems special."

"Doesn't she, though? She looks it too." I bit my fist and controlled my dick from hardening at the thought of her. Aella was soft on the eyes, heavy on the heart.

I wanted her.

And in more ways than I typically wanted a woman. I was interested in her mind more than her hypnotizing body.

Saved by a phone call, I pulled my ringing phone from my pocket and smiled at my sister's face on my screen. She'd snapped a photo of us from my phone and saved it as her contact picture for whenever she called me. Her bright smile took over the photo. It overshadowed me. She made the photo what it was.

"What's up, baby girl?" I answered her call.

"Hey, bro. I miss you. How are you?"

I smirked. "How much do you need, Layla?"

"Dang. I can't just call my brother, tell him I miss him and ask how he's doing?"

"Of course, you can. But you don't. So how much?"

"Four-hundred dollars for a new camera," she admitted. Film school was more expensive than I assumed it was.

"Four hundred for a damn camera?"

"That's actually cheap," she said. I brushed my hand over my face and chuckled.

"I'll take your word for it," I said. "I got you, though. I'll send it to your account when we get off the phone."

"Thank you so much." She squealed. "You're the best brother ever."

"Shit. I better be."

After we disconnected our call, I sent what

she needed with priority. Layla was a good girl. She deserved the world and I was the man to give it to her. I would kill anyone who hurt her physically or emotionally. After all the hell we'd been through in our lives, we deserved peace. Especially Layla. She deserved all the good I could give her.

I called Aella when my nerves settled. I'd never been this thirsty in my twenty-seven years of living. Aella was a different breed. A beautiful mystery that I wanted to unfold.

"Stop doing that!" She shouted. She answered the phone yelling at her brothers. "Hello?"

"Good evening, beautiful."

"Evening," she simply said, but I could hear the smile in her voice. She couldn't fool me.

"We still on for tonight? What's a good time for you?"

"I really want to, but I don't know if I can. I don't have a babysitter and Josh has a lot of homework that I want him to focus on."

"We don't have to go anywhere, Aella. I'm cool with chilling at your crib."

"What makes you think I want a bad boy like you in my house?"

"Bad boy?" I scoffed. "Damn, baby. That's how highly you think of me?"

"Are you denying you're a bad boy?" She asked. Her emitted seductive and teasing.

"Pretty much. There's more to me than that, beautiful. Give me a chance to show you before you assume the worst about me."

"Your game is tight."

"I'm not running game, woman. You don't have to worry about that with me."

"I'll take your word for it," she said.

"Good. Because I would never lie to you or steer you wrong."

"We'll see," she said. "Eight o'clock is fine with me."

"See you at eight," I said and hung up.

Contemplating ways to woo her took over. Impressing her was my main priority as I looked out the window and rolled it down to enjoy the slight breeze of Albany.

Tonight, was going to be a night to remember for us both. I planned on staring in her face as she rambled about whatever she wanted to. Just listening to her speak and looking in her beautiful face would do me a lot of good. Aella had no idea how long I'd had eyes on her. It was fine time I held her in my arms.

"You sure you ready for that?" E glanced in

the rear-view and asked. I nodded eagerly. If only he knew how ready I was to see her again. To have more of her in more every way possible.

"I'm ready, E. Been ready to call her mine."

"Do what you gotta do to bag her," he said. E understood me better than anyone else. I was sure he could spot the arrogance in my eyes. Whatever I wanted, I got. And I needed Aella.

Chapter Three

Aella

"Is that what you're wearing?" Danielle looked me up and down with wide eyes. After mentioning that Tyree had asked me out on a date, she was over my house twenty minutes later to get the details face to face. She even offered to take care of my brothers for the night. Danielle refused to take no for an answer.

"Is there something wrong with it?" I rushed to the full-length mirror in the corner to analyze myself. The short black dress that stopped in the middle of my thighs fit me snuggly. I'd found the gem hanging in the back of my closet. Along with the thigh-high lace sandals I had on.

"It's sexy," she said. "Too sexy."

"You think he might get the wrong idea or something?"

"Hell yes. I know I would."

I laughed and shrugged. "Maybe I want him to. A man like that isn't used to being turned down. He won't be getting any of this kitty tonight."

"Have you seen him? I don't know if I would turn him down either," she giggled.

I turned around to look at her and shook my head. "I'm going to tell Desmond on you."

"You can try." She rolled her eyes. "He's always too busy to hear it."

I walked toward my friend and pulled her in my arms for a hug. She cherished the ground her boyfriend walked on, but he hadn't had time for her lately and it was taking a toll on her.

"I'm sorry, Danielle. I know your love life is in question right now. Have you talked to him at all today?"

"Girl." She waved the subject off, then pulled away from me. "I don't even want to talk about it, Aella. I just know he is going to lose me and he will regret. Won't be any turning back once I'm gone."

"I don't blame you." I nodded to prove I understood where she was coming from.

"Now back to you. Tyree isn't going to know how to act once he sees you in this. I'm going to take the twins back to my house."

"You sure? Josh is hanging over one of his friend's house for the night."

"Yes, I'm sure. You need to have fun. Unless you want me to stay upstairs with them? Will you be okay alone with him?"

I smirked at my friend and went underneath my bed for the protection I'd stored there after my parents were killed. "There's one in every room," I explained. "I won't go down without a fight."

Danielle's mouth fell open. "I see you, bad ass."

"I'm just trying to protect my brothers," I said. "I'll do whatever I need to do to protect them."

Having a gun used to scare me. Now I had no less than five of them around the house. It was sad that I didn't feel safe in the neighborhood I grew up in. After what happened to my parents, I didn't trust a soul on the block.

"I'm going to pack the twins up, so we can get going," Danielle said. She talked about my seven-year-old brothers like they were two years old instead.

"Thank you for this, Dani. I really appreciate you." We hugged once more before she skipped out of the room, excited to bond with my brothers for the rest of the night. I usually hated to leave them with anyone else. They didn't like being around people after everything we'd gone through, but Danielle was family. They loved her like she was their sister too. They were comfortable around her.

I paced back and forth in my room upstairs until the front door slammed down below. My phone vibrated on the nightstand near the bed. The butterflies in my stomach showed out. Without having to look at my phone, I knew it was him. Tyree Lawson was calling me. He would be coming over tonight to hang out and that still blew my mind.

"Hello?" I answered with a whisper, then cleared my throat.

"Sup, beautiful. We still on, or are you standing me up?"

I covered my mouth to stifle my giggles. He brought out the teenage girl buried deep inside of me.

"What's so funny?" He chuckled.

"I thought about standing you up, but we're still on."

"Oh, that's cold-blooded. Would've had a nigga crying himself to sleep tonight."

"Who you think you fooling?"

"I'm outside," he blurted, bypassing my rhetorical question. The Apple Watch on my wrist stated he was twenty-minutes early. "I couldn't wait anymore," he concluded.

Tyree had me smiling from ear to ear and I didn't understand it. His charm was effortless.

"You don't have to. I'll be down in a minute,"

I said, then disconnected the call.

His deep voice already had my knees buckling. I glided down the stairs with ease, careful not to miss a step. Smoothing my hand over my dress, I reached for the doorknob then drew back. My hesitancy wasn't because I didn't want to see him. It was because I was nervous to spend too much time with him. He wasn't the type of man you could just forget. Tyree's dominance spoke for him.

Finally, I grabbed the doorknob and turned it to allow him access. Tyree pulled flowers from behind his back and handed them to me. The gesture shocked me and swooned me at once.

"Thank you." I blushed. "Come in." Tyree stepped in slowly and closed the door behind him. "Make yourself at home. I'm going to put these in water." I smiled until I disappeared in the kitchen and took a deep breath. I was twenty-five and had never been on a date of any kind. My parents made sure I was focused on the bigger picture. I always promised my dad I would finish college before I took a man serious. Tyree was the first date I'd accepted. I couldn't explain why.

"Thought I was going to have to go looking for you," he said when I reentered the living room. Tyree was standing in the middle of it, facing the kitchen's threshold.

"Why didn't you?" I teased. I learned quickly that it was the wrong thing to do. He approached me with a handsome smirk upon his face.

"Don't tempt me to react before I think, Aella. I already feel I'm moving too fast with you."

I nodded while eying his lips. No other words emitted. Only mesmerized stares exchanged between us.

Tyree moved in for the kill, and I backed up, afraid to take the bait.

"I..."

"No, it's my bad," he said and dropped his head. "I just been waiting to be this close to you. I'm fucking up already."

"Waiting?"

"Yeah. I told you I've seen you around, Aella. You've caught my eye over a thousand times."

"You never spoke."

"Believe it or not, I'm a shy ass nigga around beautiful women. You're beyond that, so how you expect me to act?"

I blushed uncontrollably. Tyree knew what he was doing. He was a charmer that could clearly make any woman soaking wet from his sweet talk.

"I expect you to step it up for me." I walked around him, knowing he would follow. Backing me against the nearest wall, he trapped me by putting his arms at both sides of me.

"Challenge accepted," he said.

Tyree rubbed over my cheek with his thumb. Nestling his head against my neck, he kissed my spot gently, sending chills down my spine. I wondered how he even knew how to touch me so delicately. How did he know exactly where my spot was? Obviously, he was dangerous. Tyree knew how to captivate me with his words, his touch, and now his lips. Beyond moving too fast, I just knew we wouldn't be able to stop any time soon.

A moan accidentally escaped my lips. Once it did, he moved his lips from my neck to my lips. He planted his lips firmly against mine and rested them there for what felt like a beautiful lifetime.

I pushed him back when it became too much. Not because I wanted it to end, but because it was my first official kiss. I'd never been intimate with a man before. I was embarrassed to tell him.

"Tyree... I've never..."

"I know," he said. He held my arm and led me to the couch. "I've looked into you. I've done my fair share of research. No one can say they've had you. You're a good girl. You're all about your family."

"Should I be impressed or freaked out?" I wondered aloud.

"Both." He chuckled.

Before I could restrain myself from doing anything I may regret later, I sat next to him and cupped the side of his handsome face. His eyes roamed my face, then returned to my hazel eyes.

"Kiss me again," I said. "It'll be my second kiss."

Tyree waited until I nodded to confirm what I wanted. During my nod, he leaned in and smashed his lips against mine. Bliss overwhelmed me. Regardless of how fast we were moving, it all felt right. Like this was meant to be. Almost like we were meant to be. Maybe I was overthinking it. I'm sure I was. Despite how rapid my thoughts and emotions were, it still felt right.

Tyree's fingertips traveled over my soft thighs and I didn't mind it. His touch felt familiar despite being so new to me.

"Aella," he broke our kiss to speak. "I don't want you thinking that I only want one thing from you. I like kissing you and I know damn well I can please you, but I want more."

"More?" I whispered. He'd just gotten here, and he was already talking about wanting more with me. I wished he would pinch me. This was all too much. My first kiss was with a man my parents would've never agreed with. Tyree was a bad boy. Perhaps a gangster or thug. But right now, he was gentle, soothing and careful with me.

"You heard me," he said. "But we'll get there," he assured. It was a statement that told me he wouldn't give up on what he wanted.

"Did you eat?" he asked.

I shook my head and smiled. Smiling around him was inevitable and clearly contagious. He matched my expression and stood from the couch. I followed suit when he offered his hand to help me up.

"What are you in the mood for?" He held on to me. The affection made me feel more than wanted. I felt... secure.

"I'm not picky," I said.

"Yeah, well, you should be."

Tyree pulled my dress down for me, situating my attire. After leading me to the front door, he watched me lock up and guided me to his two-door, candy painted Charger.

"Your brothers?" he asked as he disarmed his car and opened the passenger door for me.

"They're safe. Josh is with his friend. I talked to the parents so don't worry."

"I know where Josh is," he said.

"It's not enough to stalk me. You stalk my brother too?"

Tyree laughed and shook his head. "Yeah. Basically," he joked seriously.

He closed the door once I was tucked safely inside of his car. Truth be told, I didn't care where he took me, long as I was with him.

"How late can you stay out tonight?" he looked at me and asked after he joined me inside. "If you leave it up to me, you won't be back until tomorrow afternoon."

"You better make it worth my while."

Tyree revved his engine and chuckled. "You talk a lot of shit, you know that?"

I only looked at him, taken aback by how much of a gorgeous man he was.

"I fuck with it," he gripped my chin and said.

I was glad I'd given in to spending time with him. Tyree wasn't all bad. In many ways, he surpassed good. I was up for the task of exploring him.

Chapter Four

Tyree

Aella belonged on the passenger's side of my ride. I never thought I would see the day she would be this close to me, though. Seeing her around town and wishing she was mine was different than actually taking that leap and having her with me. I was one step closer to bagging her.

"You serious?" She looked at me crazy and interrupted my thoughts of her.

"What? I asked you what you wanted to eat, and you act like you couldn't choose." I chuckled. We'd pulled into the parking lot of one of my favorite BBQ restaurants. It wasn't a five-star venue, but if I knew Aella as well as I assumed I did, she didn't want all that anyway. She wasn't flashy. She was a simple girl who appreciated the little things. I loved that about her.

"I love this place," she said. Every time she

smiled, it made my day. At this rate, she could get whatever she wanted out of me.

"I thought you would. I've spotted you here once while I was eating. You were with your brothers." I killed the engine, then got out to help her out the car.

"Okay. You're starting to creep me out a bit," she stepped out and said.

We were face to face. Too close for me not to lean in and kiss her cheek.

"I don't want to creep you out," I pulled back and said. "It's just hard not to notice you."

"Tell me about it." She walked around me and giggled. "Let's eat." She summoned me along. Aella had no idea what she was getting herself into. If it was one thing I loved, it was a woman who could eat.

"Let's," I agreed.

The view from behind was impeccable. Her ass bounced slightly with every step. I jogged in front of her to catch the door. Aella rubbed her hand across my stomach as she thanked me and walked inside.

"I'm going to freshen up in the bathroom before we're seated. You should join me."

My face revealed my shock as I followed her. Her mood had shifted, and our sex appeal had strengthened. Aella led me to the family restroom. Inside it was dark until she cut the light on and locked the door.

"I can't resist anymore." She sighed. Rushing in my arms, she stood on her toes and met me half-way for a kiss that had her moaning in my mouth. I thought twice about grabbing her ass until my hands roamed there on their own. Smashing her body against mine, she wrapped her arms around me and held me as close to her thick body as she could. She smelled like lavender and I wanted to know how she tasted too.

"Aye, woman." I backed her into the bathroom wall. We both knew that shit wasn't sanitary but that couldn't stop us either. Once she got us going, it was hard for us to stop. "You're making it real hard for me to control myself around you."

"Maybe you don't have to."

She was talking big shit like she wasn't a virgin. She'd never gone as far as she had gone with me, and that was saying a lot about her. She was different from the women I was used to fucking with.

"I want to," I whispered in her ear.

Aella smiled like I'd passed a specific test. After washing our hands, we snuck out of the bathroom acting like nothing had happened. A few glances in our direction had her giggling until we reached the hostess and requested a table in the furthest corner away from everyone else.

"So... a virgin, huh?" I asked soon after settling across from her.

"Yup." She shrugged. "Let me guess. You don't believe me?"

"Why would you think that?" I side-eyed her while opening a menu to skim through and kill time. I knew exactly what I wanted. I got the same BBQ platter whenever I visited the restaurant.

"Men usually think I'm lying if I mention it during a conversation. Hell, everyone usually thinks I'm lying. But when men try to talk to me, I like to throw that out there because I know they usually only want one thing."

"That's not always true, beautiful."

"Maybe not for you," she returned promptly.

"Definitely not for me," I corrected. I could

get pussy from anyone I wanted. Women threw that shit at me every day. Aella offered more. I could tell she was different by the way she carried herself. She was focused on something bigger than the bullshit happening around her every day. She only wanted to provide a better life for her brothers now that her parents were six feet under.

"So what you're a virgin, Aella? It's admirable, and it says a lot about you, but I'm still here, shawty. That shit won't run me away."

"Good," she whispered. "I don't want you to go anywhere anytime soon."

Aella batted her lashes and stared at me with a seductive expression that made my dick jump. I couldn't deny how badly she triggered my raging hormones. The only thing I could do was control my dick around her until she was ready for me to go deep. However long she wanted me to wait it out, I would.

"I want you to stay off the streets, Aella. You and Josh. I know you don't know me like that and maybe you don't trust me just yet, but it aint safe out there for y'all."

"I know," she said. I didn't expect it to be that easy, but I was glad it was. "We should be okay for a while and when the funds get low I'll just get another job. We'll be okay. I know my parents wouldn't like me out there. It took you bringing him home for me to realize he'd been watching me. He only wanted to help. Thank you for not hurting him."

"Do you think I'm some type of monster or something?" I chuckled. "He's a kid. I would never hurt him. And you don't need another job, Aella. You work enough. Trust me, I see how hard you are working for them. Whenever you fall short, I'm here. Just let me be here for you."

She was noticeably stubborn and didn't trust

a soul outside of her brothers, but I could handle that. Soon, she would trust me beyond a shadow of a doubt too.

***

"This better be good!" I stormed through the door of the trap and glared at everyone in attendance. "I had to stop what I was doing to come here. Explain!" I didn't care who explained the reason I had cut my time short with Aella. I only knew the reasoning better had been good.

Aella and I were getting to know each other. She was starting to open up to me and answer every question I asked her. She was giving in to the details I needed to know about her. Just when the going was getting good. I mean really fucking good! I got a call from E that trouble was going down on my streets. Trouble brought too much attention to the blocks I controlled, and too much attention brought the police along. I wasn't having that.

"A shoot-out happened on Clarkson an hour ago," Trent spoke up. It was always Trent speaking up. I respected that about him. Even when he looked frantic and shook to stand up for himself against me, he still did it.

"Who sent the shots?" I asked.

"We think Key and his people did," he said. My nostrils flared at the sound of my rivalries' name. I'd assumed we laid our drama to rest months ago. Apparently, we hadn't if he was still shooting at my people.

"How do you want it taken care of, boss?" E looked at me with anger taking over his face. He was the last person I wanted to place in any danger. I didn't want him engulfed in my feud. Key had an issue with me. We used to be friends and because I parted ways due to not liking the way he called the shots, he wanted to get back at me for leaving his side. I was once his right-hand man. His pride had taken a serious hit when I left his side and built my own team.

"I'll handle it," I said.

"You can't handle it alone," Trent said.

"I said I'll handle it!" I shouted. With no idea what to do next, I left out of the trap and headed for my car. If it meant keeping my men safe, I would assure them I had it all figured out, even if I didn't. This was my fight, not theirs.

"Wait up, Ty," E shouted and chased me out. His big body was jogging toward me when I looked back. E was all over 300 pounds. His height of six-seven made him look like a giant.

'I don't want to hear it, E."

"You gon hear it," he said. "You're my brother, man. Key and his people keep gunning for you. They won't stop until they get your attention."

"I told you I would take care of it."

"You don't think I know you better than that? I know you don't have a plan, Ty. Let me help you figure this out."

"I can't do that, E. If something happens to you then that blood is on my hands. I can't let it go down like that."

"It won't." He patted his chest. "I can handle mine. We can take them niggas if they keep coming for us. You know I would put my life on the line for you, boss."

"I know you would. That won't be necessary, though. I don't want that for you."

"Ty…"

"Just let me figure it out," I interrupted him and said. "Trust me, aight?" E nodded slow, then dropped his head. "Stay safe tonight. I'll hit you in the morning, E." With that, I got in my car and sped off down the road.

Funny how my life was in trouble and all I could think of was protecting Aella and her family. I had to think of something quick. If I was being watched and they went after the woman I couldn't stop thinking about, all hell would break loose on my end.

I wanted to drive back to her house to see her. It was going on ten at night, and I was still craving her presence. I hadn't gotten enough of it. The only thing that stopped me was my overbearing fear that I was being watched and possibly followed after the news I received. I punched my steering wheel and headed for my condo. I'd given Aella a long talk about being safe and staying out of the streets and now I was in a whirl of my own trouble. Thankfully, my sister was safe. She was over a hundred-thousand miles away at college, doing her own thing. I was grateful she couldn't be located or touched.

Just because I couldn't see Aella, didn't mean I couldn't call her. The moment I got in, I planned to hit her line and confess how much I missed looking into her pretty face already. Beating me to the punch, she'd called me the second my tires drove around the driveway of my condo. When she was around, all was well. Aella had me wrapped around her finger already and she didn't even know it.

"Missing me already, huh?" I answered the phone chuckling.

"Maybe," she cooed. "And I'm calling to check how you're doing. Is everything okay?"

"Yeah," I lied. I would hate myself for making her beautiful ass worry about me. "Everything is everything. I'll have to make that up to you. I'm sorry I skipped out early."

"I'm sorry you did too. I like being around

you. You'll definitely have to make it up to me."

"What do you have in mind, beautiful?"

"Surprise me," she whispered.

Lord knows I couldn't wait to do that.

Chapter Five

Aella

At two in the morning, I awakened with my face on top of my phone. Light breathing was coming from the other end of the phone, causing me to smile. Tyree and I were on the phone for hours before we fell asleep on each other. I'd probably fallen asleep first, but it didn't matter. I was glad he was still around. Grateful he was still on the phone with me. I never thought this would happen to me. I was free falling and it was sickening yet I couldn't stop now if I tried.

"You good?" he asked. His deep baritone shocked me.

"I thought you were sleep," I whispered.

"I'm a light sleeper," he said. It made sense. A man of his caliber had to watch his back at all times.

"I see," I quipped.

"Now answer my question, woman."

"I'm fine, Tyree."

"That you are."

"Stop it." I covered my face and blushed like he could see me.

"Tell me what's on your mind," he said. "I can hear it in your voice. I know it's something."

I wondered how he did that. How did he know? My brothers were on my mind. I worried about them every second of the day, especially when we were away from each other. It was two in the morning and I couldn't stop worrying if they were okay. Although I knew they were. They were in good hands. I'd made sure of it, but I still couldn't stop myself. It was inevitable after everything we'd been through.

"My brothers. I worry about them a lot. I

still think about my parents and miss them so much every day. I wonder what they think about and if they are truly okay."

"I understand," he said. His deep tone was soothing. I could listen to him talk all night if he'd let me. "My sister is off at college living her best life. She only calls when she wants money for a new, expensive gadget." He chuckled. "I know she gets down about our circumstance sometimes. We come from nothing and our parents are locked up. It's natural, Aella. I'm sure your brothers think about your parents and what happened just as much as you do. The thoughts do not fade no matter how much time passes. It only gets easier to handle, but they'll never forget what happened. They'll be okay because they have you, and because they have each other."

"Thank you." I sighed.

"For what? What I do?"

"I needed to hear that. All of that. Even the part about you," I said.

"I'm here now, Aella. You better utilize me, girl."

"Don't tempt me. I would hate to burn you out," I joked seriously.

"Do your thing. I don't think I'll mind being used by you."

Tyree was sweeter than I would've ever imagined he could be. He was a street dude. Though he was rough around the edges, he was soft with me and I really appreciated it. He had no idea how much I appreciated him for that.

"Are you this sweet to all your women?"

"You are something else." He scoffed. "There's only you right now. You're the only woman I'm interested in. But naw, a lot of women have called me an asshole in the past."

"So why me then?"

"How many times do I have to tell you, Aella? You're special. I've peeped it for a while. You're hard to miss and I'm glad I didn't. Glad I spotted you."

"What took you so long to talk to me if you've been watching me for so long."

"I was waiting on the perfect opportunity, but I learned that there's no such thing. Then I found Josh on the corner and knew I had to bring him to you. I wasn't happy we had to meet under those conditions, but I'm grateful I was able to bring him home to you."

"Me too. The thought of something happening to him just…"

"Nothing will happen to him. Trust me. I got y'all," he promised.

Thankful I was off the next day, I threw

myself back on the bed and smiled.

Having my time consumed by him was a good pastime. I appreciated his undivided attention to every detail about me.

"You should get some sleep," he said.

"Don't go." I cringed when I said it. I'd started out a little mean to him, merely wanting to protect myself from being hurt in any way. Now, I was pleading with him not to hang up the phone.

"I'm not going anywhere, beautiful. I'll be here."

He'd distracted me from overthinking my situation tonight. Usually, I was up all night, stressed and sad over things I couldn't change. Tyree was a glorious distraction.

"When can I see you again?" he asked. Little did he know, he didn't even have to ask.

"The choice is yours, Ty."

"Ty, huh? Who said you could call me that?"

"I'm sure you don't mind it."

"I don't. You'll be calling me other things soon." His seductive tone was the only clue that I needed to understand what he meant.

"Come over for dinner tomorrow," I said.

"It's a date," he responded quickly.

Tyree had taken over for my bad dreams tonight. For that, I was indebted. Dinner was the least I could do.

***

My brothers were back. They were out of school and free from their after-school programs. Besides that, neither of them was trying to hear me out about having Tyree over for dinner.

"Why that nigga gotta eat over here?" Josh

said. I looked him upside his head in awe. His mouth had gotten really reckless since our parent's demise.

"Excuse me? What have I told you about your mouth, Josh?"

"I'm just saying. Why he gotta eat over here? He can eat anywhere in the world. Why over here?"

"Is that the man who bought J home the other day?" One of the twins asked. I nodded and kissed his cheek before turning to Josh with a scowl.

"Because I invited him," I said. "You should behave yourself and be nice to him after what he's done for you."

"What he do for me?" Josh scoffed.

"He got you out of trouble. He brought you home before something bad happened to you, or worse. Go wash up and get out of my face, Josh. Prepare for dinner. And help your brothers wash up, too."

Josh mumbled things under his breath. Storming out of the kitchen, he stomped up the stairs until I threatened to beat his ass. He was worse than me when it came down to trusting others. We weren't close to other members in our family and he was closed off from everyone else. I tried to change that about him. I tried my hardest to get him to interact with more children around his age, but I couldn't force people onto Josh. He would have to get over this phase on his own timing.

I sighed and held back tears while checking on the meal I was cooking. My mother would've suggested I showed out. She would've told me there was no half-stepping when I was trying to impress a man with a good meal. Soul food was on my mind. Collard greens, fried chicken, macaroni and cheese and yams were on the menu. I had an hour left before he would be knocking on the door and I was wondering if I should add anything else to the menu. Baking a cake was in question.

"It smells good as hell in here," Danielle startled me when she spoke. I turned around to her standing in the doorway licking her lips.

"You just don't knock at all anymore, huh?"

"For what, girl? You gave me a key to access your abode whenever I wanted."

"Big mistake," I murmured.

"I'm sorry?" She put her hand on her hip and slanted her eyes at me. "What'd you say?"

"Nothing. Would you like a plate to go? Tyree is coming over for dinner tonight. I'm introducing him to the boys.

"After one date?" she questioned me, but I expected that. Tyree and I knew we were moving a little fast. Too fast. But if he was going to be around, he needed to interact with them. He'd already met Josh. Something told me Tyree would be around for a while. And even if he wasn't, I wanted my brothers to know who I would be hanging out with at times.

"Pretty much," I said.

"Aella, you need to be careful." Danielle sighed.

I stopped stirring the macaroni to focus on her instead. "Let me get this straight. You encouraged me to go on a date with him, and now you're telling me to be careful? What changed?"

"I wanted you to go out and have some fun, but then…"

"What Danielle? What changed?"

"There was a shoot-out last night," she blurted. "The streets him and his boys be on was shot up because they are beefing with another group of men or something. I don't fucking know, okay! It's hard keeping up with everything going on in the hood. All I know is, it was on the news and everyone is talking about it. Tyree is trouble, and even if he isn't, he's associated with trouble."

"What time last night?" I asked.

Danielle shrugged. "Around eight or nine, I think."

I dropped my head and huffed. It was around the time he'd told me he had to go. We'd finished dinner and stopped at the lake to walk around the beautiful trail that surrounded it. The conversation we were having was so good and insightful. It broke my heart when everything was cut short due to an emergency phone call. Tyree made sure I got in safe and sped down the road like a bat fleeing from hell. I knew something bad had happened in his world. I just didn't expect that it was along the lines of something this deep.

"Shit," I cursed under my breath.

"I'm sorry, Aella. I didn't want to be the one to tell you about this but with everything that has happened with your parents, I don't want you to get sucked in a world like this. You can't handle another incident like…"

"I know, Danielle," I interrupted her from finishing. "I know."

"What are you going to do?" She approached me and rubbed my back.

"I'm going to talk to him about it after dinner. I have to."

"I agree. You should talk to him about it. And yes, I would like a plate to go," she added. Danielle knew how to ruin a moment with laughter. This time, I was grateful she did. I needed to laugh to keep from crying. I could move on from Tyree in a flash. I wasn't the type of woman who remained stuck on a man, but this news reminded me of my parents.

Last night, he'd promised to protect me and my brothers. He'd offered to help us whenever we needed it. And now, it seemed his life was in danger.

Just when I was starting to get to know him, trouble in his life was unfolding. After one day with him, I'd started to care for him. This wasn't fair. The lessons in my life were unclear. Sometimes I felt I was losing everyone around me in the most tragic ways.

"Are you okay?" Danielle asked, pulling me out of my detrimental thoughts. If she wasn't there, I would've shut down and cancelled dinner.

"Yes. I'll be okay," I assured her.

Chapter Six

Tyree

I hadn't saw her beautiful face since last night. She had me phoning E to ask him if it was too soon to miss her this early on. He told me what I already knew. That I was in over my head and needed to slow down. The difference between me and him was, he hadn't experienced her the way I had. He didn't know how special she was. I did.

Parking alongside the curb of her two-story, childhood home, I killed the engine and grabbed the bags from my backseat. I couldn't attend dinner empty-handed. Desert was on me. A cheesecake, apple pie and vanilla ice cream accompanied me. I gave options to satisfy everyone.

I knocked on the door, anxious to lay eyes on her again. Her hazel eyes captured my attention every time, but her lips always took over. They were pink and glossed; tempting and luscious.

Aella opened the door with a faint smile etched upon her face. "Hey. You're just in time. Come in."

Something was up with her, I could sense the tension in her sweet voice immediately.

"You good?" I asked after shutting the door behind me and trailing behind her. Her posture was different, too. Aella was sadly mistaken if she assumed I wouldn't notice she was vividly on edge about something.

"Yup. I'm fine." She nodded without looking back to face me. She was avoiding my eyes for reasons unknown and I didn't appreciate that shit.

"What's up y'all?" I let it go for a moment to greet her brothers. The younger twins accepted my dap and greeted me warmly, but Josh didn't budge.

"I thought we were cool, man," I said.

"Yeah, we were. That's before you tried to bag my sister."

Aella cleared her throat. "Josh," she grilled him.

"It's all good," I told her. I looked at Josh with remorse. I understood exactly where he was coming from. I would be the same way if I was in his shoes. "I'm trying to do more than that. I can't say bagging her isn't the ultimate goal, but that's not all I'm trying to do. I'm trying to get to know y'all too."

The twins smiled up at me as Josh's disdain softened. They followed his lead. It was obvious they looked up to him.

"Can I get a chance, man?" I opened my arms and waited for his answer. Josh nodded slowly, but the pace didn't bother me. I was just satisfied with the chance he'd given.

"Alright." Aella smiled. "Let's eat. I got to keep y'all handsome men fed."

I chuckled at that. Shawty was really smooth with her shit. Smoother than me at times.

"Oh, you hooked it up like that?" I praised her skill. Aella had the dining room table set and filled with a lot of dishes. Steam floated above every dish lined in the middle of the table. "Damn. I could get used to this. This all for me? Who else coming?"

"Boy sit down so we can pray over this food." Aella giggled. "It's for all of you," she said. The cold shoulder feeling I felt from her when I first arrived was fading. She was starting to give me a much warmer welcome.

"Bet." I smirked and sat across from her. We held hands over the table as she prayed. While everyone's head was down, I looked up and smiled at her beauty. While she thanked God for the food.

I thanked God for the opportunity to be around her right now. Yeah, it was becoming that deep for me.

"Amen," everyone finished and lifted their head in unison.

"Amen," I joined their union a second later.

"Let's eat," Aella chimed. There was no other placed I rather have been.

The stress that was weighing heavy on my mind was vanishing. She was bringing out the best in me, forcing me to leave the trouble behind. With her, it was nonexistent. The chaos outside of everything we had going on didn't matter.

"How was everyone's day?" she looked between all of us and asked. Neither of us answered right away. All the men surrounding her looked at her with a bright smile on their face.

I waited until their answers were out of the way before responding. It felt good listening to them tell her about their day. They looked toward her with endless respect. Her brothers admired her being. They looked at her like she was their entire world.

"What about you, Tyree? How was your day?" She stopped chewing to stare at me intensely. She stared at me like she was waiting on me to tell her something she already knew. I was good at picking up on vibes. Something was on Aella's mind and I couldn't wait to ask her about it later on.

"My day was productive," I leaned back in my chair and said. After shrugging, I leaned forward again and reached for her hand. "It's better now. Now that I'm with you."

"I'm glad you're here," she whispered. On one hand, she was upset with me about something. And on the other hand, she was genuinely happy that I was in attendance.

"Get a room. Please." Josh scoffed and rolled his eyes.

"My bad, man." I chuckled. "We don't want to ruin your meal."

"Good." Josh sighed in relief. He regretted speaking once the attention was directed to him. Aella had asked about his grades and he'd frozen up about his grade in math.

I watched Aella speak to him. She was stern, but she still spoke to him with so much love.

"Josh, your grades are important. School is…"

"Important. I know, sis. I'll do better," he interrupted her and said.

"You damn right you will." She nodded vigorously while speaking. "Because I will shut all the fun you have down. Boy you still have it made without mom and dad being here. You better be grateful."

"I am," he mumbled. Josh sounded disappointed that he'd let her down. I was impressed by her effortless will to take care of things. Inside and outside of her home, she was in control. Slowly, but surely, she was gaining control of my heart.

***

The boys had cleaned up and went to their rooms for bed. I grabbed Aella's wrist and gently pulled her into my arms when she returned downstairs from seeing them to bed.

"Is there something up with me and you?" I asked. I knew there was. Hopefully she wouldn't try to lie to me. I thought too highly of her to endure that on her behalf.

"You tell me," she said. She tried to escape my arms, but there was no use. I wasn't letting her go no matter how hard she tried to get away from me.

"Aella. Keep it real with me. Things were great between us last night. I had to leave you early, but I thought we left off on good terms. We even talked on the phone all night."

"Tyree, what's going on out there? Am I going to lose you before I get the proper chance to have you?" she asked. That shook me up. I didn't know how much she knew about the chaos going on around me, but I knew she knew something.

"You need to keep it real with me," she spoke against my chest, then rested her head on it with a deep sigh.

"I'm going to take care of everything. You don't need to worry." I wanted to ask how she knew. I wondered who put the bug in her ear, but I knew it didn't matter. She only wanted answers. She didn't want to discuss anything outside of that.

"Tyree..."

"Aella. I said I was going to take care of it. There's no need for you to worry about me. I can take care of myself."

"Yeah, well, so can I. But you're still here and I'm willing to let you in. You have to let me in too. You can't put yourself in a position where I could lose you."

"I'm not." I dropped my head. She clearly didn't understand that it wasn't me who was the problem. I was being targeted by hating ass niggas that wanted me out of the equation altogether. "Just believe me when I tell you I'm not going anywhere. You don't have to worry about losing me."

"Don't lie to me," she shouted. The outburst startled me. She was upset. Tears formed in her eyes as I was taken aback.

"Aella. Are you listening to me?"

"Yes, I am. I hear you. But I know how the

streets can be. My parents died on the sidewalk right in front of me. All we were doing was taking the groceries out of the car. I left them for one second and came back out to them bleeding out on the sidewalk. I'm not going to deal with that from you."

Breaking down in my arms, she buried her face in my chest and wept for moments that felt like a lifetime.

"Why are you crying?"

"This is too much, Ty. I like you, but I can't let anyone put me through that again. My parents didn't know what was going to happen to them. If you can let this life go to protect yourself, then you need to."

"I don't need any protecting, Aella. How many times do I have to tell you that I'm okay. I'll be good."

"Promise me," she said. Aella's tears were

breaking me down. In this moment, I would give her whatever she wanted. Whatever she needed.

"I promise, beautiful," I leaned down to whisper in her ear.

Our lips connected firmly. I invaded her mouth with my tongue and indulged in her sweet taste. Aella moaned softly against me. My dick poked her stomach, wanting to be freed to have at her.

"It's all good to trust me, Aella," I assured her.

"I hope so." She wrapped her arms around me. Aella held my arm and guided me to her bedroom. Placing her index finger over her lips, she instructed me to remain quiet until we made it into her bedroom.

Emotions were high between us. I wasn't happy she knew the truth about my dilemmas in the streets, but I was relieved she did. She kissed me like it would be the last time she would be able to, and I kissed her like it was the first time each time the chance was presented to me.

"I don't know what you're doing to me already," she whispered against my lips. I laid Aella on her queen-sized bed and hovered over her. Grateful for the light shining above us, I admired her striking features in awe. She was so fucking beautiful. Nothing like you see in a magazine. She was much more stunning than all that. Her beauty was a mystery. It left me wondering how God could have created something so special for the world to have. With her, I was on some lover boy type shit. I'd been waiting around for these little moments. I'd dreamed of her many nights, wondering if she was the one for me because after seeing her one time I couldn't shake her image in my head.

"Promise me you won't worry, Aella," I said. Kissing from her neck, down to her chest, I inhaled her scent and felt completed.

"I can't do that," she whined underneath me. Her body reacted to every touch. Aella trembled underneath me, then wrapped her arms around my neck to hold me close.

"I'm always going to worry about you. Let me. It's normal. Means I care about you," she said. I didn't need any more convincing after that. I let her have her way because she was right, and I cared about her too.

In the heat of the moment, I managed to ease her pants off of her. Once they were to her ankles and tossed across her bedroom, I roamed her thick thighs with a smirk on my face. Her silky brown skin looked delicious. I was hurting to taste the treat between her thighs.

"Spread them for me," I leaned in to whisper in her ear. While moaning, she obliged quickly. She parted her thighs and took a deep breath. "Can

I?" I asked, needing her permission before I dug in to feast on her sweet treat.

"Yes," she cooed. Music to my ears.

Chapter Seven

Aella

"Yes," I cooed. I'd given him permission to taste me. Less than a minute later, his head was planted between my thighs. Tyree kissed my inner thighs so gently my body buckled. The anticipation was too much as I awaited his warm tongue on my clit. "Oh, God," I moaned. I hated to call on our Lord and Savior, but it was impossible not to.

Tyree licked my slit, then circled his tongue around my pussy lips. The light teasing around my clit turned me on. If I wasn't afraid of the hard dick poking through his pants, I would've pleaded for him to take me. I would've begged him to push deep inside until he was out of good dick to give.

"Tyree." I rubbed over his low-cut haircut and moaned. The feeling was magical. One of the best feelings I'd ever encountered.

Tyree gripped my thighs while tasting me.

He squeezed firmly and groaned against my pussy like I was the best thing he'd ever tasted.

"There you go," he said when I moved my hips. Tyree held his tongue in place as I moved my hips and rotated them to my liking. On the brink of losing my mind, I squealed when an orgasm ripped through me.

"I'm not done with you," he whispered against my pussy, driving me even more crazy.

"Tyree," I whined. I tried running from his tongue, but he wasn't having it. He switched our positioning quick. Lying on his back, he lifted me on his face and instructed me to hold on to the top of my headboard. He massaged my ass cheeks as I rode his face. Trying my hardest to be quiet, I covered my mouth with one hand and bit my palm to refrain from screaming out in pleasure. I couldn't believe this was happening. I'd opened up to him in more ways than one.

"Cum for me again," he spoke from underneath me. Tyree was loud with the way he was tasting me. He slurped every juice that flowed from me like he was thirsty for me.

My body convulsed on top of him. After two mind-blowing orgasms, I couldn't take anymore. I pleaded for mercy until he laid me next to him and pulled me in his arms.

Tyree kissed my forehead. I grabbed the side of his face to taste myself from his lips. It was the most passionate kiss we'd ever shared at this point. Our kiss became as intense as his tongue lashings on my clit was.

"Turn over," he said. It emitted like a demand. Though I was scared of what would happen next, I followed suit and did as I was told.

"Tyree," I called him. I wanted to warn him to be careful with me. I had no idea what came next.

"Relax," he whispered in my ear after I switched onto my back. His hands massaged my ass. Tyree was good with his hands. My body relaxed under his spell. The tension I'd built up was diminishing by the minute.

"Tyree!" I screamed his name when his tongue entered my asshole. He tried his hardest to convince me to relax like this wasn't anything new to me. The things he was doing to me were taking me under, attaching me to him sexually. Beyond getting to know his mind, his tongue had gotten really acquainted with areas I'd learned was my spot.

He would hardly let me touch him. Tyree held my hands down, so I couldn't stop him. He focused on pleasing me as he counted my countless orgasms. Every time I thought my body was spent and I could no longer take anymore, he demanded another body-quaking orgasm from me that blew my mind.

"I'm staying with you tonight," he advised me in my ear.

"Did you think I was going to let you leave?" I questioned him.

Now that he was here, I wasn't letting him go anywhere.

***

"You're leaving?" I woke up in the middle of the night to him searching for his shoes in the dark. The streetlight outside of my window invaded my blinds. A streak of light entered my bedroom and provided enough light for me to see him scanning the room for his things.

"Business," he said.

I looked at the clock next to my bed. It was three in the morning and he was leaving.

"At three in the morning?!" I shouted.

"Lower your voice, Aella. Don't wake the boys."

He was right. I did need to lower my voice. I didn't even want the boys knowing he'd spent the night with me. Josh would have a damn fit.

"Where are you going at three in the morning, Tyree. What business do you need to handle at this time? It can't wait until morning."

"Look, I just got a call so I gotta skip out, aight? I'll be back." He kissed my forehead when I approached him. On his heels, I chased him down the stairs, pleading with him to be safe.

"I'm always safe, beautiful. Keep it tight like that until I get back. I can't wait to taste you again." With that, he was out of the door. From the screen door, I watched him hop in a black escalade. The car was waiting for him to get inside. It sped off the moment he got in.

After shutting the front door, I locked it and

braced my back against it. I prayed to God he would be okay. The feeling in the pit of my stomach was unsettling. For the life of me, I couldn't shake it. Something was terribly wrong. Tyree wouldn't admit it to me because he wanted to protect me. Truthfully, he didn't have to admit it. I knew there were things I didn't know. His lifestyle was deeper than I thought it was.

I gasped when Josh walked out of the kitchen. He had a bottle of water in hand and was heading back to his bedroom. "You okay?" he asked.

I only shook my head, surprised that he didn't say more or ask anything more besides that.

"I don't think you have to worry about, Ty," he said. "He's well respected. Everyone in his team will do whatever they can to protect him."

I sighed and put my hand on my hip. "And how do you know all this, young man?" I questioned him in return.

"I just know." He shrugged. "See you in the morning." Jogging up the stairs, he disappeared into the first visible door on the hall. He shut his door quietly behind him, leaving me alone with my tortuous thoughts.

Tyree had just left, and I already wanted to call him and ask if he was okay. If he would've let me, I would've gone with him. I wasn't being needy or territorial, I just wanted more for him. His story wasn't that different from mine. Though his parents were alive, he still didn't have them around to be there for him.

I wanted to be the shoulder he needed. Of course, he had his sister, but I wanted to be another available for Tyree.

The stairs were too much for me to take on right now. Settling for the couch, I laid on it and stared at the ceiling, restless. Sleeping wasn't possible. I wouldn't be able to sleep until I knew he was okay. Until I heard his voice again, I wouldn't be able to properly function.

The way Tyree took care of me sexually without having to enter me took over my mind. I could still feel his tongue roaming my body. Hearing him groan as he pleased me was the ultimate turn on. He got off on making me cum over and over again. He chuckled when I cried and whined his name from the immense pleasure. The most shocking part of it all was, I wanted to give myself to him entirely. If it had gone that far, I wouldn't have regretted it no matter the outcome of our new fond connection. In every way, I wanted him. There was a thirst I needed to quench timelessly until I got enough of him.

Unable to shake my thoughts of him, I got up and went upstairs in search for my phone. Texting him a reminder to be safe was pivotal. My thoughts were taken over by him now. Worrying about him physically hurt. Knowing he was still intact would bring me peace.

The way Tyree took care of me sexually without having to enter me took over my mind. I could still feel his tongue roaming my body. Hearing him groan as he pleased me was the ultimate turn on. He got off on making me cum over and over again. He chuckled when I cried and whined his name from the immense pleasure. The most shocking part of it all was, I wanted to give myself to him entirely. If it had gone that far, I wouldn't have regretted it no matter the outcome of our new fond connection. In every way, I wanted him. There was a thirst I needed to quench timelessly until I got enough of him.

Unable to shake my thoughts of him, I got up and went upstairs in search for my phone. Texting him a reminder to be safe was pivotal. My thoughts were taken over by him now. Worrying about him physically hurt. Knowing he was still intact would bring me peace.

Tyree: I'm okay baby girl

Tyree's response came through quick.

Tyree: Don't worry

A double-text from him made me take a deep sigh of relief. Lying underneath the comforter on my bed, I buried myself under my pillows and closed my eyes. My head was spinning just as fast as my life was moving. Different events were happening back to back, however, this one hit different. Encountering him was random yet much needed. He'd given me a new outlook on things. Tyree didn't know how much he meant to me already.

Already.

The way he handled Josh's attitude at dinner and introduced himself to my brothers warmed my heart. Despite the news Danielle had told me, I couldn't remain upset at him or the situation he was downplaying. I was too busy being swooned by his attentiveness to our needs.

Tyree was the man of the hour. I prayed he didn't drop the ball. Most of all, I prayed nothing bad would happen to him.

Chapter Eight

Tyree

"It's handled," E said when I got in the car.

"Handled?" I looked at him from the backseat, through the rear-view mirror. His eyes were dark and glossy. He had a conniving smirk on his face that had me on edge. "What did you do, E?"

"Me and the crew took care of them niggas. We sprayed their blocks and tagged majority of them."

I brushed my hand down my face. He clearly didn't understand what this meant. He'd basically started a war. Killing people wasn't the answer. No matter how many times the opposite side targeted us, retaliating wouldn't help our case.

"Why'd you do this without my consent, E.

You know I fuck with you, but that shit was sloppy. I can't celebrate that with you."

"It's all good. Because it's handle," he said. "It's been hours since we took care of it. No one is shooting back. Everything is calm."

"Yeah. The calm before the storm." I scoffed. I had a bad feeling about this. Key and his people wouldn't just lay down and take the heat. They would apply pressure right the fuck back. I knew him like the back of my hand. We used to run the street thick as thieves. No way he was going to let this slide without making sure I paid for it somehow, someway.

"Fuck!" I punched the back of the seat and grumbled.

"Ty, calm the fuck down. I just told you we handled that shit for you. Have I ever let you down?"

E had never let me down. He'd become my

right-hand man and he always made sure everything was taken care of and in order for me. He would do whatever I asked of him. Still, this situation was sticky, and complicated.

"Naw, you haven't," I simply answered. All I could do was hope for the best. If we got through the day without any complications, then we were good. Maybe he did take care of it.

"I came and got you because I think you should steer clear of Aella today. Just for today. When the day is over, and they haven't come for us, then we're good, boss."

"Yeah. I appreciate that. I would hate to put her in any line of fire."

"I already know. What's up with y'all anyway?" E looked back and forth from me, to the road. He was headed in the direction of my condo to drop me off.

"Circle the blocks for me first, E. I wanna

check shit out."

"I got you." He nodded.

"As for Aella. I don't know." I chuckled just thinking about her. She made me feel good, and so did thinking of her. Thinking of her always brought a cheesy ass smile to my face. She was softening a nigga with every interaction with her.

"Feels good to be around her. I haven't felt like this in a long time."

"Shit. I'm glad this is finally happening. You been checking her out for too long. You always bitched up when you saw her, scared to talk to her n'shit." He laughed.

"Aye, man. Watch your mouth," I warned him and laughed. "She just…"

"Special? Yeah nigga, I know. You say that about her all the time."

"Alright then. So you know what it is. Aella

special as fuck. She makes me feel something. She makes me want something better than all this shit. Fuck the money. She makes me want to aim for more than that, you know?"

"Wow." E shook his head. "What the fuck is going on? She got you sprung like that already?" He clowned me.

"Already," I repeated and nodded. "I can't wait until this shit is over to get back to her. When night falls and it's still calm. I'm gon find my way right back to her. If something happens to me, make sure she straight, aight?"

"I feel you, boss. You can't fight a feeling like that. You gotta make it back to her. Nothing is going to happen. Trust me."

I agreed with a nod. The conversation ended as I overlooked the blocks. I checked that everything was good as we checked on our men serving on the block.

"Aight, E. Take me home," I said.

***

As promised to myself, when it all died down, I made it back to her the next morning. As promised to her, I was safe, without a scratch or scuffle. Her brothers were already off to school, and she was preparing for work.

"I have to go to work," Aella said. She tried walking around me to get in her car, but I wasn't having that.

"Hold on." I held her in my arms, refusing to let her go. "Why you in a rush to escape me like that, woman?"

"Tyree, I was worried sick about you all night. Do you know how that makes me feel? It doesn't feel good." She pouted.

"I apologize for that. It won't happen again, aight? My men took care of things."

"What does that even mean?" She huffed.

"It means I'm here. You see me, right? I'm right here." I held her chin, forcing her to look at me. "Act like you see me, shawty."

"I do see you," she admitted. "It's hard not to."

"Good." I towered over her short ass and smirked. "Now call out for me. You know you want to."

"Excuse me?"

"I'll give you more than you would make there in a day. Just hang with me today."

"Tyree…" She sighed again. This time, a beautiful smile was attached to the end of it. I had her right where I wanted her.

"Fine," she gave in quickly like I knew she would. "Doesn't mean I want your money. I just want to be with you."

"And you'll get the money anyway." I kissed her cheek.

I looked her up and down, impressed with how her body filled out the uniform she had on. I couldn't wait to take it off her. To taste her again. I swiped my tongue across her bottom lip, then kissed it.

The sound of her giggles filled my ear until gunshots replaced it. Gunshots rang behind us, dragging her down the block as people screamed and ducked for cover. I covered her as we ran toward the steep stairs that led to her porch.

My focus was on the front door as I carried her up the stairs, shouting for her to stay down and tucked underneath me. Before I could get her inside, a powerful, burning force took me down. A bullet struck my back, tackling me to the ground as my body weakened on top of her. Tires screeched as the car sped off down the street, then the sound of Aella's screams blocked my hearing until I drifted asleep.

Epilogue

Aella

I stood in the middle of the waiting room in shock.

I'm sorry ma'am, Tyree didn't make it.

The doctor's words traumatized me, taking me back to the day the emergency responders told me my parents were dead on the scene. This couldn't have been happening again. He promised! He said everything was fine! He claimed it would all be okay!

Tyree's friend, E, stood by my side. I leaned on him for support before I fell over. Processing the news was harder than it should've been. I mean, I hardly knew Tyree like that. Our connection was new, but I felt like I'd known him for a long time. He was stripped away from me. Killed in front of me. I'd held him and screamed his name until he took his last breath. His last words to me were an apology I didn't deserve. An apology I would have to pass on to his sister away at college.

"Noooo," I screamed and fell to my knees. E picked me up and led me outside of the hospital. He tried to calm me down by telling me it would all be okay, but I didn't believe him. Tyree had told me the same thing. In fact, he'd promised me it would be okay. And it wasn't. None of this shit was okay anymore. He was dead. My city never gave life. The streets of Albany only sucked the life out of people.

"It wasn't supposed to happen like this," E said. Seeing a man cry was intense. Tears fell from his eyes. He wiped them away quick and looked toward the sky like Tyree was already up there, looking down at us.

"Let me take you home so I can go take care of this."

"No!" I shouted at him. "Haven't you learned anything? Your friend is dead. This won't solve anything. They'll just come after you next."

"I don't care!" he shouted back at me. "Tyree was all the family I had, and now he's gone. I have to get back at them niggas for taking my dawg away from me like that."

I stormed away from E. I wasn't going to be associated with that. It hurt to lose Tyree, but I still had my little brothers to live for. I couldn't lose my life behind this. I couldn't let them suffer alone and lose their sister too.

"Tyree wouldn't want this," I spat as I walked away.

E grabbed my arm and dropped his head. "You're right. Please just let me take you home. He told me to make sure you were straight if anything ever happened to him."

I looked E in his eyes as tears cascaded

down my cheeks. "He did?"

"Yeah. He said you were special and that you made him feel things he never felt before. Said he wanted something bigger than money because of you. You made him look at life differently, Aella. I think he was thinking about leaving the game for you."

My heart shattered in pieces. He'd been taken away from me before he could make a change on his own.

Anger started to mask my pain. I saw red as fury overwhelmed me. I stared at the blood on my hands in horror. Tyree's blood covered me. His death would forever haunt me because he'd faded in my arms. He tried speaking before he gradually drifted away from me. I'd begged him to hold on. I pleaded with him to wait until the ambulance arrived. I had faith he would be okay until he let go. He'd tried to fight to stay alive for me, but the pain was too powerful to bare. The bullet had struck his lung, piercing a part of him that couldn't be recovered.

Tyree had gotten something that he didn't deserve. A bullet in the back. The shooter was still out there. His face was unknown, but that didn't stop me from wanting whoever was responsible or associated with the heinous crime to be taken care of.

"Can you put security on my house? For my brothers?" I asked E.

"I'm already on it," he responded quickly. "You and your brothers aren't in this. Key and his crew got exactly what they wanted. They have wanted Ty out of the equation, so they could take over his turf."

"I want them taken care of," I said. The words coming out of my mouth astonished even me, but I meant them. That's exactly what I wanted. Everything I had previously said had gone out of the window. Something needed to be done about Tyree's demise. He was taken away from me too soon and I wasn't going to be the only one hurting at night over it.

"Whoever the fuck they are, key and his team, makes them suffer," I said. I stared E directly in his eyes without blinking. Tears stained my cheeks as I spoke with disdain in my voice.

"You sure?"

I only nodded. My strength was seeping by the minute.

"You got it, boss," he said. Tyree was a reflection of me, and I was going to finish what he enemies started.

I was indebted to him, so I owed him this much. He'd come in my life and showed me more genuine love than a man outside of my father ever had. He had potential to be greater than he was.

From the very beginning, he'd been a blessing to my family. He'd gotten Josh off the streets and brought him home to me. Regardless of the bad things he'd done in his lifetime, he was undeniably caring and always willing to right his wrongs. It wasn't fair for anyone to shorten his life with envy or jealousy of how powerful his being was.

"Make them suffer," I told E.

Hopefully, once that was taken care of, Tyree could really rest in peace.

After all the chaos he'd endured, he deserved that much. He truly deserved to finally rest without constantly watching his back. Tyree deserved endless peace.

The End

CPSIA information can be obtained
at www.ICGtesting.com
Printed in the USA
LVHW032236220120
644443LV00014B/1039